Library of Congress Cataloging-in-Publication Data

Fink, Joanne, 1954–
    Jack, the seal and the sea.

    Adaptation of: Jan und das Meer.
    Summary: Jack spends his days sailing the sea and
taking in nets full of half-dead fish, ignoring the polluted
condition of the water, until he finds an ailing seal and
receives a message from the sea itself about its sorry state.
    [1. Water—Pollution—Fiction. 2. Seals (Animals)—
Fiction. 3. Sea stories] I. Aschenbrenner, Gerald. Jan und
das Meer. II. Title.
PZ7.F49576Jac   1988   [Fic]   88-4601
ISBN 0-382-09985-0 LSB 10 9 8 7 6 5 4 3 2
ISBN 0-382-09986-9 PBK 10 9 8 7 6 5

© 1988 by Verlag Heinrich Ellermann, Munich, originally
published in German under the title *Jan und das Meer*.

© 1988 English adaptation by
Silver Burdett Press Inc.

Gerald Aschenbrenner

Jack, the Seal and the Sea

English adaptation by
Joanne Fink

Silver Burdett Press
Englewood Cliffs, New Jersey

As a small boy Jack was always out with his father, a fisherman, on his boat the *White Wind*. He grew up surrounded by the smells of fish and the sea, and the cries of the gulls. He had never thought about being anything but a fisherman.

When Jack was old enough he bought his own fishing boat. He called it the *White Wind II*, after the boat he had loved as a boy. He worked hard on his boat, fishing the same waters his father had.

Slowly though, things changed. It took Jack longer to find fish, and longer to fill his nets. The sea did not sparkle as it once had. The fish were small and sickly. Jack threw back more and more fish all the time. Many days he thought to himself, "It would take a miracle to bring in a catch like I used to." Still, Jack never thought about being anything but a fisherman.

One day Jack hauled his net on board expecting the usual catch of half-dead fish. Instead, he stared in amazement into the eyes of a little seal who lay among the silvery mackerels in his net.

"Welcome aboard the *White Wind II* little guy!" Jack said as he lifted the seal from the net. It was clear to Jack that there wasn't much life left in this seal. An oily film covered his fur and bits of debris were stuck to him.

Jack found some old towels and used them and some fresh water to give the seal a much needed bath. He picked out the best of his catch and offered them to his little passenger. Then, he went back to his work. Slowly, the seal regained his strength. By the time Jack checked on him again he could see a bit of a sparkle in the seal's big, dark eyes.

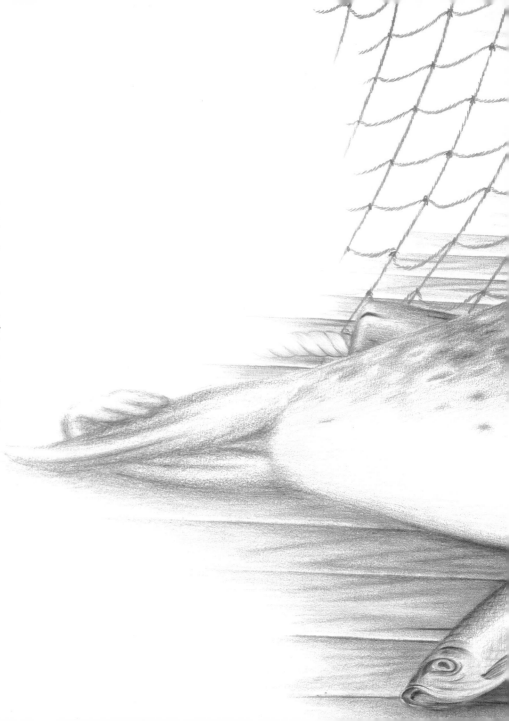

"Well, my friend, now that you look so much better what shall I do with you? I bet you'd like to go back to your friends, wherever they might be."

Jack looked in all directions, but for as far as he could see there were no seals. He started up the engine and cruised along the coastline. He checked everywhere. But there were no seals in any of the places where Jack had seen them before.

All afternoon Jack searched for seals. But it was useless, there were none to be found. Jack saw garbage scattered on the beaches, and garbage floating by his boat. "No wonder the seals are gone," he thought sadly. "Why would they want to live in this mess?"

The little seal began to get restless. "What now my friend, could you be hungry again?" Jack brought the seal more fish. He gobbled them right up, and looked around the deck for more.

"More?" chuckled Jack, "Well, if you've got that big an appetite, maybe you should do some fishing for yourself!"

Jack lifted the seal over the side of the *White Wind II*. It returned to the sea with a splash. With a flick of its tail the seal disappeared under a wave and darted away. Jack watched the animal's progress and began to worry about him. "Should I just let him go off alone?" he thought. "He'll find some other seals soon. What if he doesn't, what will happen if he doesn't?"

By now the seal was just a tiny dot bobbing in the waves. Jack stared at the little dot, all alone in the sea. "I can't let him go off like that," he decided.

Jack followed the little seal. When the boat caught up with him he had a big, silvery mackerel in his mouth. It was the biggest, healthiest looking mackerel Jack had seen in a long time. The seal gobbled the fish up quickly and caught another, and then another. Jack couldn't believe how many nice, big fish the seal was catching. ''This might be a good spot to try some fishing,'' Jack thought.

Quickly, Jack lowered his nets into the sea. The seal was still splashing around in the water, diving under one side of the boat, and popping up on the other side. Jack didn't want him to get tangled in his net again, so he lured the seal over to the boat with some fish, and brought him on board. The fisherman was happy to have his small friend back on the *White Wind II*.

Jack pulled his nets through the water with his boat. When it was time to bring them in he worked hard to pull up the first net. It was very, very, heavy. "Maybe I've caught some more seals," he thought.

There were no seals in Jack's net this time, just lots and lots of big, healthy fish! More than he had caught in a very long time. Jack couldn't believe his eyes. "What luck you've brought me today little seal!" he exclaimed.

It was late in the day by the time the nets were emptied, the fish stored, and the deck washed down. The sun was sinking in the sky, and Jack was very tired.

Jack decided to stay out on the water for the night. He settled down on the deck, with the seal by his side, and thought back over his strange but happy day. As the water lapped against the sides of his boat, and the stars twinkled in the night sky, Jack fell asleep. The sea was calm, and a soft breeze rustled Jack's hair as he slept.

Suddenly, the wind picked up, the sky darkened, and the waves grew to a frightening size. Jack's little boat was tossed in a terrible storm. A huge wave broke in front of him, the sea parted, and he heard a deep, booming voice rise from the depths. "Help me Jack! Help me as you did my little friend, the seal! I rewarded you for that, now it is time for you to come to my rescue!

"Look what has happened to me! Everything that's been dumped in me has made the fish sick. The plants can't live in me, and people are afraid to swim in me! Stop polluting the sea! If everyone will work together the sea can be enjoyed for longer than any of you will live!"

The voice faded away. The storm stopped as suddenly as it began. The stars twinkled in the night sky, and a soft breeze still rustled Jack's hair.

Bright morning sunshine and the cries of the gulls woke Jack from his sleep. The seal was nowhere to be found. Jack went to the rail and looked in the sea for his friend. Calm water stretched for as far as he could see, but there was no trace of the little seal.

He started to check his boat for damage from the storm, but stopped. "It was a dream," he said to himself, "it had to be a dream."

Jack couldn't stop thinking about his dream. He thought about it as he started up the *White Wind II's* engine, and he thought about it as he headed for port.

On his way in Jack saw bottles and bits of trash floating by his boat. He'd gotten so used to it being there that he hardly noticed it anymore. Today, it kept bringing his dream back to mind.

He remembered hearing all the talk about pollution. "I was just like everyone else, I didn't think it would happen here, to our part of the sea," Jack muttered to himself. "But I was wrong, we were all wrong, it has happened here, and we have to do something about it."

Jack docked his boat later that morning. Several friends were waiting nearby, keeping an eye out for him. Jack never kept his boat out all night, so when he hadn't returned by dusk, they started to worry about him.

Jack told them his story. They found it all a little hard to believe. But Jack was their friend, so they helped him unload his fine catch and listened to him anyway.

That night Jack gathered the villagers together in the town school. He told them how he had rescued the seal, and about the message from the sea.

Some people believed the story, others didn't. But it didn't matter to them if the sea had really spoken to Jack. It was his message that was important. They had all seen the condition the sea was in. They knew how dirty the beaches were. The fishermen had all watched the size of their catches dwindle.

"It's not our fault!" one man shouted. "It's the big companies, and those big oil tankers and ships. They dump waste in the sea."

"Don't blame everyone else." said Jack. "We're responsible, too. We have to think about what we can do to clean up our own harbor and keep it that way."

"There must be things we can do!" one woman cried. Others agreed, and before long they had a long list of ways to clean up the sea. Letters to the government and industries and new local laws to prevent the villagers from dumping garbage in the sea were just a few.

"Things will get better," thought Jack as he listened to everyone.

And then it came to him. The people in his village were not the only ones who needed to hear the message of the sea. It was time to stop fishing he decided. There was something else he had to do.

Now Jack sails the *White Wind II* up and down the coast. He stops in all the towns and villages to tell his story.

Sometimes he thinks about being a fisherman again, but not until everyone hears his message, and cares about what happens to the sea.